LITTLE ITALY

Tana Reiff

GLOBE FEARON

Little Italy

Tana Reiff
AR B.L.: 2.7
Points: 1.0   UG

HOPES *And* DREAMS

Hungry No More
For Gold and Blood
O Little Town
Push to the West
Nobody Knows
Old Ways, New Ways
Little Italy
A Different Home
Boat People
The Magic Paper

Cover photo: International Museum of
Photography at George Eastman
House
Illustration: Tennessee Dixon

ISBN 0-8224-3677-9
Printed in the United States of America

9 10 11 12 13 14   06 05 04 03 02

Globe
Fearon

Pearson Learning Group

1-800-321-3106
www.pearsonlearning.com

CONTENTS

CHAPTER 1

Southern Italy, 1920

"See here, little ones,"
said Mrs. Trella.
"Your papa is home!
Let's clean you up.
I want you
to look pretty
for your papa."
The three children
came to her.
She washed
six little hands.

Mr. Trella
opened the door.
The door was broken.
It made
a cracking sound.
Mr. Trella
did not look happy.

"So sad, so sad,"
he said.

"You will fix
the door,"
Mrs. Trella said.

"No, no,"
said Mr. Trella.
"The trouble
is not the door.
The door
is easy to fix.
The trouble
is the fruit.
I cannot sell
our oranges.
No one will buy
my oranges."

"What is wrong
with our oranges?"
asked Mrs. Trella.
"They taste sweet
to me."

"They are not
sweet enough,"
said Mr. Trella.
"The Americans
do not need oranges
from Italy anymore.
They grow oranges
in North America now.
And, besides,
our land
is wearing out.
We do not get
as many oranges
as we once did.
And they are
very small, too."

"What shall we do?"
asked Mrs. Trella.

"We must think
about going away,"
said Mr. Trella.
"We must think
about going

to America.
Our land is poor.
Our town is crowded.
Our children
will have nothing
if we stay here.
They need
a chance for
a better life.
And so do we."

"It would be
such a different life,"
said Mrs. Trella.

"We could make a living,"
said Mr. Trella.
"We cannot do that here.
And we could give
our children
hope for tomorrow."

"We do not have
enough money
to go to America,"
said Mrs. Trella.

"We can pay
for one ticket now,"
said Mr. Trella.
"I will go first.
I will work hard
and save money.
I will send you tickets.
Then you can bring
the children over."

Mrs. Trella
hated to see
her husband go away.
She did not want
to leave her home town.
She did not want
to take the children
to America
by herself.
But she knew
this might be
the only way.
This plan
might be the ticket
to a better life.

Thinking It Over

1. If you were
   the Trella family,
   would you go
   to America?

2. What do you think
   of Mr. Trella's plan
   to go first?

3. Do you think
   the Trellas will find
   a "better life" in America?

CHAPTER 2

There were signs
all over town.
Ships were looking
for people
to take to America.
Every week
a young man
came to town.
He sold tickets
to ride
on the ship.
He talked about
the streets of gold
in America.
The young man
sold Mr. Trella
one ticket.

Mrs. Trella
packed a bag
for her husband.

Her tears
fell on the bag.
Those tears
would go along
to America
with the bag.

She and the children
went into town
with Mr. Trella.
All the neighbors
came to say good-bye
to Mr. Trella.
They waved and cried.
They kissed and hugged.
They wished him
good luck.
They knew
they would probably
never see him again.

"Good-bye, my family,"
said Mr. Trella.
"I will write.
I will send you
four tickets.

You four
will come to America
very soon."

In his mind
Mr. Trella
said good-bye
to his town.
He had lived here
all his life.
He would miss
his farm.
It had once been
a good farm.
He looked back
at the mountains.
He had loved
to climb these mountains.
He remembered
the river.
He had loved
to swim in this river.
How could he
leave behind
everything he knew
and everyone he loved?

He tried
to be brave.
He hugged his family
one last time.
His heart ran over
with love and fear.

A mule cart
took Mr. Trella
to the train station.
The train
took him
to Naples.
There, he saw
the big ships.
On the dock
he bought a book.

"This book
will teach you English
by the time
you reach New York,"
the book cover said.

"It might *teach*,
but will I *learn*?"

Mr. Trella
wondered.

Someone tied
a little tag
to his coat.
His name
and some numbers
he didn't understand
were on the tag.
Then Mr. Trella
and the other people
going to America
got into a line.
They were pushed
like sheep
up a ramp
to board the ship.
For 15 long days
Mr. Trella
was on the ship.
Finally, the trip
was over.
He was in New York.
He was in America.

Thinking It Over

1. Can a person
   learn a new language
   in 15 days?

2. If you left your home,
   what would you remember
   about it?

3. Do you think
   the trip to America
   will be worth the trouble?

CHAPTER 3

Mr. Trella
stayed in New York.
He did not have money
to go past the city.
But there was work here.

There was
no farm work, however.
Another man from Italy
asked Mr. Trella
to work with him.
So Mr. Trella
took a job
in the building trade.
He learned to cut
blocks of stone.
He helped lift them
into place.
Little by little,
the stones grew
into tall buildings.

It was
very hard work.
But every day
marked one day less
until the family
could join him.
Every day
was one day closer
to a better life.
He did not think
about how hard
the work was.
He could only think
about how happy
he would be
to see his family.

Mr. Trella
spent his nights
by himself.
On the way home from work,
he ate dinner.
The food was good.
"But it doesn't taste
like my wife's food,"
he said to himself.

In his mind
he could still taste
her cooking.

   After dinner
Mr. Trella read.
He studied.
He learned
some English.
He worked
in the little book
that promised to
teach English
in 15 days.
But it took much longer
to learn
than to teach.

   He lived
on very little.
He saved
almost all his money.

   Mr. Trella
worked beside
Sal Penta.

Sal was also
from Italy.

"Come out with us,"
said Sal one day.
"We have
a good time.
Meet us tonight
at the Green Monkey."

Mr. Trella
did not know
what the Green Monkey was.
But he found
the place.
He found the men
playing cards
and drinking.
There was money
all over the tables.
There were pretty women
waiting for the men.

"How much
have you won?"
he asked Sal.

"Fifty dollars so far!
Come on, give it a try,"
laughed Sal.

Mr. Trella watched.
He didn't join
the game.

"What's the matter, Trella?"
Sal asked.
"Are you chicken?"

"I can't spend
that kind of money,"
said Mr. Trella.
"I'm saving
to buy tickets
for my family."

"So am I!"
laughed Sal.
"This will help you.
Come on, Trella."

Finally Mr. Trella
sat down.

"OK, I'll give it
a try," he said.

Mr. Trella had
very good luck.
By the time
the game was over
he had won
more than $100.

The next week,
Mr. Trella went back
to the Green Monkey.
This time he had
very bad luck.
Soon all of his money
was gone.
Sal and the others
loaned him more money.
But Mr. Trella
lost this, too.

Later that night,
Mr. Trella lay awake
in his bed.
He could not sleep.

"How could I
do such a thing?"
he asked himself.
"All the money
I have saved till now—
all gone."

He felt sick.
He knew he must not
play cards anymore.
He must pay back
the money he owed.

It took two more years
to save enough
for four tickets.
Sal Penta's family
was still waiting.

Finally one day
Mr. Trella bought
four tickets.
He mailed them
to Italy.
Then he waited
for his family.

Thinking It Over

1. Could you work
   for two years
   to buy four tickets?

2. How would you try
   to make hard work
   seem not so hard?

3. Do you think
   Sal Penta's family
   will ever come to America?

CHAPTER 4

"Who is that man?"
asked little Felice.

"That is a picture
of your father,"
said Mrs. Trella.
"You don't remember him,
do you, dear?"

"No, Mamma,"
said little Felice.

"You were too young
when he left,"
said Mrs. Trella.
"But you
will know him again.
Believe me.
He will send us
tickets to America
very soon."

Mrs. Trella
believed what she said.
But hundreds of days
had gone by
since her husband left.
She tried
to keep up the farm
by herself.
Her son, Giuseppe,
helped out.
But he was
just a child.
Sometimes she lost heart.
Would the tickets
to America
ever really come?

Then one day
the special letter came.

"My dear wife and children,"
began the letter.
"At last!
I have been
without you
for more than two years.

Now it is time
to begin our life together
in America.
I send you
four tickets.
Come join me
as soon as you can.
Come and see
this beautiful place.
Love, Papa."

"Children, children,
our tickets
have come!"
cried Mrs. Trella.
"We will see
your father soon!"

Giuseppe smiled.
But Felice and Liberta
did not understand.

"Let's dance!"
said Mrs. Trella.
She and the children
joined hands.

They danced
in a circle.
The dance made
the little girls smile.

Mrs. Trella
sold almost everything
they owned.
She packed
two bags
for the trip.
One bag
held clothes and food.
The other bag
held days gone by
and hope for tomorrow.
She carried that bag
in her mind.

Like Mr. Trella,
she and the children
went to Naples
to board the ship.
Now they, too,
were on their way
to America.

Thinking It Over

1. Do you carry any "bags" around with you?

2. Why does two years seem like a long time to a child?

3. Do you believe that things turn out for the best?

CHAPTER 5

The trip
was very hard.
The ship was packed
full of people.
The days were hot.
The nights were cold.
There was not much
to do.
The children cried.
"Be still,"
Mrs. Trella told them.
"We are on our way
to America now.
Everything
will be all right."

"Take a walk
up on the deck,"
said a woman.
Her name
was Mrs. Santo.

"Get some fresh air.
I will watch
the children."

Mrs. Santo's
husband was dead.
She was taking
two children
to America
by herself.

The five children
played together
every day.
There was not
much room
on the ship.
But the children
dreamed up games.
They sang
silly songs.

"I hope
we will be friends
in America,"
said Mrs. Trella.

"Oh, yes,"
said Mrs. Santo.
"Let's stay in touch."
She rubbed her eye.

"What is wrong
with your eye?"
Mrs. Trella asked.

"I think
some dust
flew into it."
said Mrs. Santo.

Her eye was red.
It felt
as if it were on fire.
As the days went on,
Mrs. Santo's other eye
got red, too.
Her eyes hurt her
during the whole trip.

Thinking It Over

1. Do you make friends
   when you go on a trip?

2. What can you do
   to stay well
   on a long trip?

CHAPTER **6**

"We are almost
in New York!"
called a man
on the ship.

The sun
was just coming up.
A light pink sky
was opening
the new day.

"Wake up, children!"
said Mrs. Trella.
"We are almost there!"

Everyone on board
clapped and cheered.
They raced to the deck.
They hung
over the rail
to see better.

Mrs. Trella and Mrs. Santo
lifted up
the little children.
They all looked
for New York City.

They had been
at sea for 15 days.
There had been
a bad storm
that lasted
for several days.
They felt ill
and had not been able
to eat.
Mrs. Trella had spent
much of that time
praying.
Almost everyone
felt tired and weak.
But this morning
everyone felt happy.

Mrs. Trella
was the first person
to spot land.

"There it is!"
she cried.
"There is America!
And there is
the Statue of Liberty!"
She held a child
in each arm.
"Can you see
the beautiful lady?"
she asked them.

The Statue of Liberty
seemed to stand
on the water.
Her torch
held a fire.
The sun
made her crown shine.
Without a word
she seemed to say,
"Welcome to America!
You are safe
with me."
Mrs. Trella knew
she would never forget
this sight.

"Look, children,"
said Mrs. Trella.
"Look at the lady!
Look at the tall buildings!
This is a beautiful city,
just as your father wrote
in his letters.
Your father
helped to build
those high buildings."

"It looks like
a dreamland!"
said Felice.

The ship
pulled into a big dock.
Right away
the rich people
walked off the ship.

"Don't rush out!"
a man called
to the rest.
"First, get on
that boat

over there.
You must go
to Ellis Island.
They will check you over.
Then you will come back
to the city."

When they got
to Ellis Island,
Mr. Trella
was waiting.
He picked up
his wife.
They held each other.
They jumped
up and down.
Mr. Trella
picked up
all three children
at once.
He was all smiles.
This was
a very happy morning.
The first part
of the Trellas' dream
had come true.

Thinking It Over

1. Why would people
   feel so good
   after being at sea
   for 15 days?

2. Do you think
   that rich people
   get a lot of breaks?

3. What does
   the Statue of Liberty
   mean to you?

CHAPTER 7

There was
a big building
on Ellis Island.
Mrs. Trella
and the children
had to wait
in a long line
to be checked out.
They waited
almost all day.
Mrs. Santo
and her children
were in front of them.

At last,
Mrs. Santo and her children
got to the head
of the line.

A big woman
looked over the children.

"The children
look fine,"
she said.

Next, she
looked over Mrs. Santo.
"Your eyes
look very bad,"
said the woman.
"We cannot let
sick people
into this country.
Someone may catch
your sickness.
I am sorry, but
I must send you
back to Italy."

"What did she say?"
Mrs. Santo asked.
A man
who spoke English and Italian
told her.

"Go back to Italy?"
cried Mrs. Santo.

"After the long trip?
How can this be?
Please let us stay!
My eyes
will get better.
Don't make us
go back!"

Mrs. Trella
cried with Mrs. Santo.
They held each other.
"God be with you,"
said Mrs. Trella.
Then the crowd
pushed the Trellas
away from
Mrs. Santo.

Mrs. Trella
turned and saw
a man leading
Mrs. Santo and the children
away to a ship.
The Santos
would never set foot
in New York City.

Then came
Mrs. Trella's turn.
The big woman
checked over
Mrs. Trella
and the children.
She put strong drops
into their eyes.
She pulled
their hair.
"That hurts!"
cried Felice.

"You may move on,"
said the big woman.

"Oh, thank you!"
said Mrs. Trella
in Italian.

Next, a young man
asked Mrs. Trella
many questions.
"Where were you born?
Where did you
last live?

Are you married?
Do you know anyone
in America?
Who paid your way
to America?
Where are you going?
Did you ever
break the law?
How much money
do you have?"

The questions
were hard
because Mrs. Trella
did not speak English.
She tried
to understand.
The man
seemed to
get her point.

"Very well,"
he said.
"You pass."
The young man
gave her some papers.

She held the papers
very close.

The boat
took the Trella family
back to the city.
They could see
the Statue of Liberty
behind them.
Mrs. Trella
got off the boat first.
She watched her foot
touch the ground.

"Am I really here?"
she asked her husband.

"You really are!"
he said.
"You really are
in America.
You really are
with me.
Our new life
begins today!"

Thinking It Over

1. Was it fair
   to send Mrs. Santo
   and her children
   back to Italy?

2. What is
   the most beautiful place
   you have ever seen?

3. Why did the man
   ask Mrs. Trella
   so many questions?

CHAPTER **8**

The Trella family
made their way
into the city.
Mrs. Trella could not
believe her eyes!
America
was nothing
like Italy!
There were
no high buildings
back home.
Here, some buildings
were 40 stories high.
Back home
the little streets
were clean.
Here, the streets
were big and dirty.
And the streets here
were *not*
made of gold!

Mr. Trella
took his family
to their new home.
It was a tiny part
of a big building.
The building
was on Mulberry Street.
The family
would live
in two small rooms.
The rooms
were five floors
from the street.
Mrs. Trella
looked for windows.
There were none.
The place
was dirty.
It was also very hot.

"What is the matter?"
asked Mr. Trella.
"You did not think
we would live
in a grand house,
did you?"

"No, no,"
said Mrs. Trella.
"This is fine.
We will make do.
You will see.
I will make
these two rooms
clean and pretty."

And so she did.
She cleaned up
the two little rooms.
She hung up sheets
to mark out space.
She made the place
into a home.
Still, it was
hot and dark.

Mr. Trella
worked hard
12 hours a day.
He always
came home dirty.
He often
came home hurt.

Mrs. Trella
looked at her husband
every night.
She began to think
about the tall buildings.
The buildings
did not seem
so beautiful now.

She spent
all her days and nights
helping her family.
Her job
was to make a home.
Life was not easy.
But the Trella family
was in America.
That was
all that mattered
right now.

Thinking It Over

1. Do you think
   12 hours a day
   is a long time
   to work?

2. When have you
   had to "make do"
   with what you had?

3. Do you think
   keeping a home
   is a job?

CHAPTER 9

The Trella family
went to church
every week.
Mrs. Trella
went almost every day.
She met many people
at church.

But the best thing
about New York
was the street.
There Mrs. Trella
could talk
to the neighbors
every day.
Most of them
were from Italy.
Mr. and Mrs. Trella
even knew
a few of them
from back home.

They called Italy
"the old country."
They spoke
to each other
in Italian.
They had little use
for English.

The street
was a lot like
one big store.
Men pulled their carts
into the street
every morning.
They sold fresh food
off the carts.

"I'll take
some oranges,"
said Mrs. Trella.
She still loved oranges.
"And let me have
those nice green vegetables."

She bought
her meat or fish last.

She did not want the meat
to go bad
while she talked
to her friends.

Mrs. Trella
bought fresh food
on the street
every morning.
She had no place
to store food
or keep it cold
for more than a day.

Life here
was a little bit
like the old country.
People even called
this part of New York
"Little Italy."
Mrs. Trella liked
being with people
from back home.

The street
was also like a park.

The children
played there.
They laughed and sang
with all the others.
Sometimes
they got into fights.
But mostly
they had fun.

Mrs. Trella
could leave the children
in the street.
She could go back up
to the two little rooms.
She knew
the children
were safe on the street.
Without the children
Mrs. Trella
could get her work done.
She went down
to get the children
when it was time
to cook dinner.

Thinking It Over

1. Have you ever seen
   a street like this one?

2. What is
   your street like?

3. Where you live,
   can children
   play on the street
   without their parents?

CHAPTER 10

In the next five years
Mr. and Mrs. Trella
had four more children.
Now there were seven.
First there was Giuseppe.
In America,
he was called Joe.
Next came
Felice and Liberta.
The last four
were born
in New York.
There were two boys.
Their names were
Pasquale and Guido.
Then came
a girl named Annalia.
The last child
was a boy.
His name was Dominick.

The family of nine
still lived
in two rooms.

Mr. Trella
still worked
long days
in the building trade.
Mrs. Trella
took care
of the seven children.
She cooked
three meals a day.
She cleaned
the floor.
She got them ready
for school.
Both parents
looked old
before their time.

There was no money
to buy new clothes.
The old clothes
went from one child
to the next.

Mrs. Trella
put patches
on the old clothes.

"We cannot
throw away clothes,"
she said to the children.
"Your clothes
may be old.
But they
will always be clean.
You children
will always look neat.
No one will guess
you all live
in two little rooms."

But one day
Guido came home
from school
with torn clothes.
He was crying.

"You're a big boy,"
said his mother.
"Why are you crying?"

"I got
into a fight,"
he said.

"Why?"
his mother asked.

"The other boys
make fun of me,"
said Guido.
"They call me names.
They say
I wear funny clothes.
They say
I do not look American.
I could not take
the jokes.
So I hit
one of the boys."

"You were born here,"
said Mrs. Trella.
"You are American.
Sometime in your life
you will have
new clothes.

Right now
we cannot buy you
such things.
But I don't want you
to get into fights."

"But the other boys
make me feel bad,"
said Guido.

"Don't listen
to these boys,"
said Mrs. Trella.
"Just be
the best you can be."

Thinking It Over

1. Did anyone ever make fun of you? What did you do?

2. What would you have told Guido?

CHAPTER 11

The big building
going up on 58th Street
was almost finished.
Mr. Trella
stood on a board
near the top
of the building.
The board hung
from two ropes.
Another board and ropes
lifted stones
from the street
up to Mr. Trella.
His job was to put
the stones in place.

"Just two more loads!"
shouted the boss.

The next-to-last load
came up to Mr. Trella.

"Get it closer,"
he shouted down
in broken English.
"I can't reach the stones."

"I can't get too close,"
a man called
from the street,
"or we'll hit
the building."

Mr. Trella
reached out his arm
to grab a stone.

"You almost have it!"
called the boss.

Mr. Trella
reached out more.
Without any warning
the load of stone
dropped ten feet.
Mr. Trella
grabbed the air.
His foot slipped.

"Watch out!"
shouted a man
on the street.
But it was too late.
Mr. Trella
fell off his board.
He landed on the board
that was piled
with stones.

Everyone stopped working.
"Hold on tight!"
shouted the boss.
"We're bringing you down."
Mr. Trella
could not understand
the boss's English.
He just held on
to the rope
for dear life.

Down came
the load of stone.
Slow, slow, stop.
The load of stone
hit the street.

"What hurts?"
the boss asked.

"My back,"
Mr. Trella said in Italian.

The boss
did not understand.
"He only hurt his leg,"
the boss said.

But Mr. Trella
had trouble standing up.

"Go home for the day,"
said the boss.
"You'll feel better tomorrow."

But Mr. Trella
did not feel better.
He should never
have tried to walk.
His back
was hurt very badly.

Thinking It Over

1. Why is language
   so important?

2. What is the worst trouble
   you have ever been in?

3. Do you think
   Mr. Trella can work again?

CHAPTER **12**

Mr. Trella
could not work
in the building trade
anymore.
His back hurt
most of the time.

He got a job
making paper flowers
for very low pay.
He worked
in a building
up the street.

The family
moved into that building.
There, they lived
in three rooms.
They had two windows.
But it was still
a small place.

The whole family
helped to make
paper flowers, too.
But every night
the children studied.
"It is very important
to do well in school,"
Mrs. Trella would say.
"I want you
to make something
of your lives."

And every day
Mrs. Trella still looked
into her second bag.
This was the bag
full of days gone by.
She talked about home
with the neighbors.
They loved to talk.
But they never left
Mulberry Street.
Little Italy
was the only part
of America
they knew.

Thinking It Over

1. How is
   Mr. and Mrs. Trella's life
   better in America?

2. What happens
   when people live
   only with their own kind?

3. What do you think
   would make Mrs. Trella happy?

CHAPTER **13**

Summer was the time
for the big church *festa*.
It was just like
festas in Italy.
People carried
tall candles
down Mulberry Street.
They pinned money
to the church door.
They put up a string
of colored lights.
They hung
flowers and flags.
They played games
and ate lots of food.
At night
they set off fireworks.
They sang and danced
on the street.
Mr. and Mrs. Trella
danced, too.

"We do not dance
often enough,"
said Mr. Trella.

"When is there time?"
asked Mrs. Trella.
"We are too busy
with the family."

"Our children
are growing up,"
said Mr. Trella.
"Soon there will be
just you and me again."

"I miss Felice,"
said Mrs. Trella.

"But she is fine!
She has made us
a grandfather
and grandmother,"
said Mr. Trella.

"Oh, yes,"
said Mrs. Trella.

"I hope
there are many more
beautiful children
to come!"

"And look how well
our Joe is doing,"
said Mr. Trella.
"He lives
in a nice place uptown.
He works
in an office.
He has
a fine wife.
I am happy
for him."

"Pasquale and Guido
are helping
to put up
those tall buildings,"
said Mrs. Trella.
"Just as you used to.
They work hard.
They will do well
for themselves."

"And Liberta
and Annalia
are working
in that factory,
making clothing.
They will marry soon,"
said Mr. Trella.
"Then they
will be gone, too."

"I can't believe
our little Dominick
is in high school,"
said Mrs. Trella.
"Time goes by
so fast."

All of a sudden
the music
got very loud.
"My favorite song!"
said Mr. Trella.
He grabbed
his wife.
"Let's dance away
the night!"

Thinking It Over

1. Do you believe
   there can be good times
   even when life is hard?

2. What is
   your favorite song?

3. Would you
   be glad or sad
   if your children
   grew up and left home?

CHAPTER 14

The years went by.
It was 1958 now.
Dominick
was the only child
still at home.
And tonight
he would graduate
from high school.
Next year
he would be going
to college.
He was
the best student
in the class.
He would give
the class speech.

Mr. and Mrs. Trella
dressed up to go
to the school.
They watched

for Dominick.
There he was,
walking up front.
He wore
a black gown.
On his head
was a flat hat.

Dominick spoke
to the crowd.

"My parents
have worked hard,"
he began.
"They have had
seven children.
Every one of us
has finished high school!
My parents are
simple and good people.
They want
nothing more
than to see their children
do well.
I am glad
my parents

came to America.
We must all
thank our parents."

Mrs. Trella
wiped the tears
from her eyes.
"He's a good boy,"
she whispered.

Mr. Trella
took his wife's hand.
"They are all
good children,"
he whispered back,
"thanks to you."

At home that night
Mr. and Mrs. Trella
sat down together.

"Our children
have moved
past Little Italy.
Maybe now
it is time for us

to move, too,"
said Mr. Trella.

"Little Italy
is fine with me,"
said Mrs. Trella.
"My friends are all here.
This is my home now."

Many years
had gone by
since Ellis Island.
Seven children
grew up.
Mr. and Mrs. Trella
were not young now.
They were still
poor people.
They still worked hard.

But their dreams
had come true.
They had given their children
a better life.
They were happy
to give that gift.

Thinking It Over

1. Could you be happy
   just knowing
   you had given
   a better life
   to your children?

2. What is your idea
   of a good life?

3. Was the Trella's hard work
   worth the trouble?